MOO LA LA!
Cow Goes Shopping

Stephanie Shaw & Becka Moor

SIMON & SCHUSTER
London   New York   Sydney   Toronto   New Delhi

Pete filled Cow's trough with water.
He fluffed her straw and set a bucket
of grain nearby.

"There you go, Cow," said Pete. "I'm going to do some errands in town. I'll be back by milking time. Come on, Dog, jump in the truck and let's go."

"*It's not fair,*" bawled Cow. "I never get to ride in the truck. *Moo hoo!*"

"Think about it, Cow," said Pete. "It's a long ride in the back."

But Cow insisted she sat in the front with Pete and Dog.

"*Sour cream!*" she mooed. "*Are we there yet?*"

When they got to town, Pete told Dog and Cow to wait in the truck.

"I want to get away before that parade traffic hits. I won't be long. I need to buy some shoes for Horse."

MOO 1A 1A

"**What?** Horse has shoes?
I *never* get to have shoes," bawled Cow.

"*Moo hoo! I want shoes toooo!*"

"Think about it, Cow," said Pete.
"You might not like shoes."

"Moo la la! I want those!"

Cow pointed a hoof at the shoe shop window.

PARADE TODAY

It took a bit of doing, but Cow squeezed into two pairs of glittery red high-heels.

They had cute peep-toes, but they pinched her hooves until her eyes watered.

"*Sweet yoghurt in the morning!*"
Cow bellowed.

"*How does Horse stand these things?*"

"Let's move along now, Cow, the streets are filling up," said Pete, "and the missus wants me to buy some dressing for Turkey."

"*How come?*" asked Cow.

"Well, we always dress the turkey for dinner," Pete replied.

"Mooo hooo!" bawled Cow.

"Then I want a dress too!"

She wobbled along until she came to Moomingdales Department Store.

"Good afternoon, Madame," said the sales assistant.
"Might I interest you in a nice floral dress? It's even
called a muumuu. It would be divine on you!"

"Nooooooo!" said Cow. *"J want that one!"*

"Think about it, Cow," said Pete. "It looks a little . . . ah . . . small."

"But J want it," mooed Cow.

So a crew of salespeople buttoned, hooked
and zipped Cow into the dress.

"*Hole-eee cheese on a cracker!*" gasped Cow.

"How does Turkey breathe at dinner let alone eat!

I can hardly moooooove!"

"We **really** need to get going," said Pete.
"I just need to get some shears to trim sheep's coat."

"*What?* Sheep has a coat? What kind of coat?"

"Well, wool, of course."

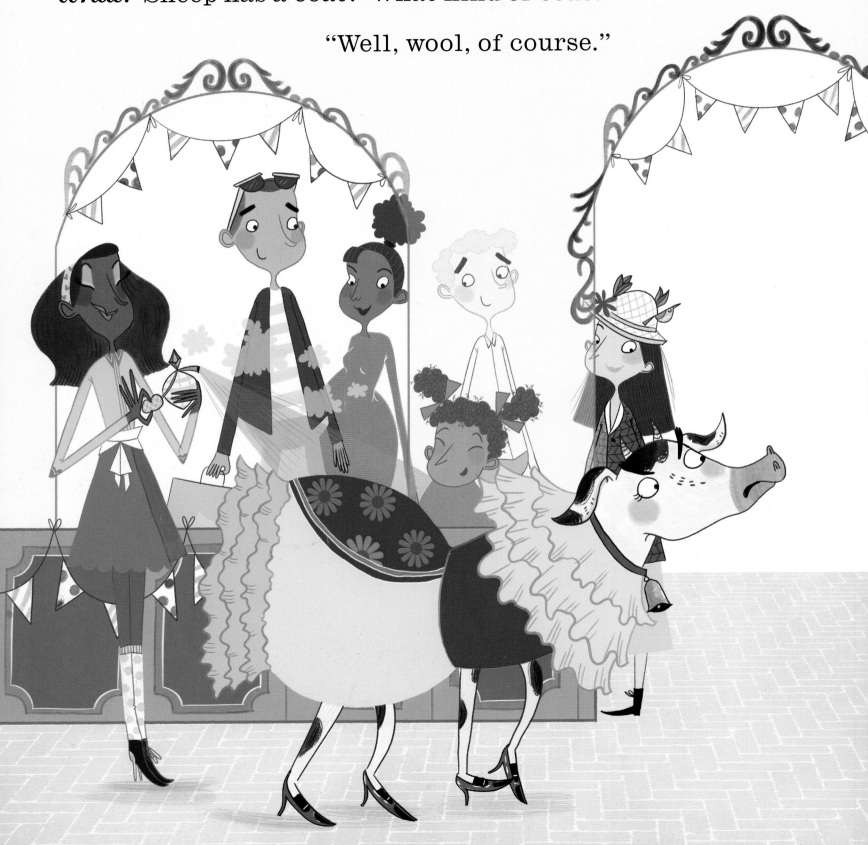

"*Moo hoo! Then I want a wool coat!*" said Cow.

"No, Cow. Trust me. You will not like it," said Pete.
But Cow stamped her hooves and tossed her horns.
"*Moo hoo! I need it! I want it!*

I have to have it!"
she yelled.

And with that she charged up the escalator and stampeded through the china department.

She only stopped when she came to a whole flock of wool coats.

PARADE TODAY

"Moo la la! I want that one!"
she said, pointing to a coat that already
had another wearer.

She tottered out of the shop in her brand new coat.

"Merciful milkmaids!" she bellowed.

"*This thing itches my hide!*"

"Cow, that's it. We **must** move along," said Pete.

By now Cow was too tired to climb into the front of the truck.

As Pete drove through town, the traffic slowed.

"Moo hoo!" cried Cow from the back.

"Mooo hoooooo!

My hooves hurt!

This dress is too tight on my tummies!

And this coat is mmmmmmiserable!"

The people lining the pavements stared and pointed as Cow slowly went by.

When they reached the town square,
a woman rushed up to Pete.

"Oh my goodness!" she gushed. "You win the prize for . . ."

Best Dressed Bovine!

But when the rosette was placed on Cow's neck,
it was the final straw.

Her knees buckled. Her eyes rolled and she fainted.

When she woke up she was back on the farm.

Pete filled her trough with water, fluffed her straw and set a bucket of grain nearby.

"Oh Pete, I was so *foolish*," said Cow.

"I'm going to stop asking for things I don't know anything about."

"I'm glad to hear that, Cow," said Pete.
"Now get some sleep. I need to put a ring on Bull."

"What? Bull has a ring?"

"Think about it, Cow," said Pete . . .

"You might not like it."